Y0-CBZ-248

The Frog and the Ox

and Other Fables

Compiled by Vic Parker

Gareth Stevens
PUBLISHING

Please visit our website, **www.garethstevens.com**. For a free color catalog of all our high-quality books, call toll free 1-800-542-2595 or fax 1-877-542-2596

Parker, Vic.
The frog and the ox and other fables / compiled by Vic Parker.
p. cm. — (Aesop's fables)
Includes index.
ISBN 978-1-4824-1312-0 (pbk.)
ISBN 978-1-4824-1256-7 (6-pack)
ISBN 978-1-4824-1457-8 (library binding)
1. Fables — Juvenile literature. 2. Aesop's fables — Adaptations — Juvenile literature.
I. Aesop. II. Parker, Victoria. III. Title.
PZ8.2 P37 2015
398.2—d23

Published in 2015 by
Gareth Stevens Publishing
111 East 14th Street, Suite 349
New York, NY 10003

Publishing Director Belinda Gallagher
Creative Director Jo Cowan
Editorial Director Rosie McGuire
Designer Joe Jones

ACKNOWLEDGEMENTS
The publishers would like to thank the following artists who have contributed to this book:
Cover: Natalie Hinrichsen at Advocate Art; Advocate Art: Natalie Hinrichsen, Tamsin Hinrichsen;
The Bright Agency: Marcin Piwowarski; Frank Endersby; Marco Furlotti; Jan Lewis (decorative frames)

Printed in the United States of America

CPSIA compliance information: Batch CS15GS: For further information contact Gareth Stevens, New York, New York at 1-800-542-2595.

Contents

The Thirsty Pigeon

There was once a pigeon who had flown for many miles without water. She was desperate for a drink, but could not find a lake, a pond or even a puddle to sip from. Suddenly, she noticed a goblet of water painted on a signboard. The pigeon had no idea that it was only a picture, so she flew towards it excitedly. BANG! She crashed right into the signboard,

4

then slid to the ground, her head spinning.
After that, the silly pigeon learnt to always
take more care.

Enthusiasm should not
outrun being cautious.

5

The Two Crabs

There was once a mother crab and her child, who lived on the seabed. The mother crab took great care to teach the little crab good manners and behavior.

One day, the mother crab said that she would take her little one up to the seashore as a treat. "But you must be on your best behavior," she

said. "I don't want all the land creatures thinking that we sea creatures are common."

"I will try, Mother," promised the little crab.

So up, up, up they went, until they reached the sandy shore. Once there, they decided to go for a stroll.

They hadn't gone far when the mother crab hissed at her child, "You are walking ungracefully. You should try to walk forwards without twisting from side to side."

"I will try," said the young crab. "Please show me how, and I will follow you."

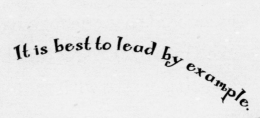

It is best to lead by example.

The Man
and the
Satyr

Long, long ago, creatures called satyrs, which were half-man, half-goat, lived alongside humans.

One bitterly cold winter's night, a man had lost his way in a deep, dark wood. As he was trying to find his way home, he stumbled across a satyr who was gathering firewood. The satyr was kind and helpful. As soon as he discovered that the man had lost his way, he asked him back to his own house.

"You can stay with me for the

night," the satyr offered. "I will guide you out of the forest in the morning."

The man gratefully accepted the satyr's offer and went along with him to his little wooden hut. As they walked through the forest, the satyr noticed that the man kept raising his hands to his mouth and blowing on them. "I hope you don't mind me asking, but why do you keep doing that?" asked the satyr.

"My hands are numb with the cold," said the man, "and

my hot breath warms them up."

"I see," said the satyr thoughtfully, and continued leading the way to his home.

The little wooden hut wasn't much further on, which the man was very glad to see. Soon the pair were both inside in the warm, and the satyr put a steaming bowl of porridge before the man, who happily picked up a spoon to eat. But when he raised the spoon to his mouth, he began blowing upon it.

The satyr looked puzzled. "May I ask why you are doing that?" he said.

"Well, the porridge is too hot, and my breath will cool it," explained the man.

To the man's great surprise, the satyr suddenly stood up, opened the door, and bundled him out into the cold and dark.

"Out you go," said the satyr.
"I'm not sure what you are, but I
will have nothing to do with you. If you can blow
hot and cold with the same breath, you must be
dangerous."

"But... but... but..." the man tried to explain,
but he was talking to the door.

Never trust a
changeable person.

The Horse and his Rider

There was once a young man who fancied himself to be a good rider. One market day, he saw a fine-looking horse for sale and was determined to ride it. He did not know that the horse had not been properly broken in, and he didn't think to ask. He just climbed a nearby fence and dropped onto the horse's back, regardless.

The second the horse felt a rider's weight in the saddle, it set off at full gallop,

with the young man hanging on for
dear life.

One of the rider's friends saw him
thundering down the road. Surprised, he
called out, "Where are you off to in such
a hurry?"

Gasping for breath, the young man
pointed to the stallion, and replied, "I have
no idea — you will have to ask the horse."

Act in haste and you will have to go
along with the consequences.

The Man, the Boy, and the Donkey

There **was once a man** and his son who were on their way to market with their donkey. They walked along the road, leading the donkey behind them, minding their own business. After a while a countryman passed by them and shouted out, "You fools, what is a donkey for but to ride upon?"

The man looked at the boy, and the boy looked at the man, and they both said, "Why, he is right!" So the man put his son on

the donkey, and they went on their way.

A little while later they passed a group of men and they heard one of them say, "Look at that lazy youngster! He allows his poor father to walk in this heat, while he rides on the donkey. Shame on him!"

The man looked at the boy, and the boy looked at the man, and they both said, "Why, he is right!" So the man ordered his son to climb down, and he got on the donkey himself.

They hadn't traveled much further when they passed two women. One woman pointed at the man on the donkey and shouted, "Shame on that lazy lout, making his poor little son trudge along while he rides on the donkey."

The man looked at the boy, and the boy

looked at the man, and they both felt rather confused by this. The man thought for a while, uncertain of what to do next. Eventually, he pulled his son up before him on the donkey so they could both travel in comfort, and they carried on with their journey.

By this time they had come to the town, and passersby began to jeer and point at them. The man stopped and asked what they were pointing at. One man said, "Aren't you ashamed of

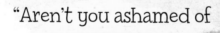

yourself for overloading that poor donkey?"

The man looked at the boy, and the boy looked at the man, and they both got off the donkey at once. They stood wondering what to do. They thought and thought, until at last they took a pole, tied the donkey's feet to it, and raised the pole and the donkey to their shoulders. They went along amid the laughter of all who met them until they came to a bridge. Then the donkey, getting one of its feet loose, kicked out and broke free. Off it ran, never to be seen again by the man or his son.

"That will teach you," said an old man who had followed them along the way. "You can't please everybody."

Please all, and you will please none.

The Frog
and the Ox

Once upon a time, a young frog was sitting with his father by the side of a pool. The pool was shady and cool, and the frogs were sitting happily among some rocks. They watched for passing flies, minding their own business and chatting to pass the time.

"Oh Father," said the little frog. "I have seen such a terrible monster! It was as big as a mountain, with horns on its head, and a long tail, and it had hoofs divided in two."

"Hush, child, hush," said the father frog,

"that was only Farmer White's ox. It isn't so big either — it may be a little bit taller than I, but I could easily make myself quite as broad, just you see." With that, the frog blew himself out, and blew himself out, and blew himself out.

"Was he as big as that?" he asked.

The young frog looked and thought for a second. "Oh, much bigger than that," he said, shrugging his shoulders.

Again the father frog blew himself out, and blew himself out, and blew himself out. Then he asked his son if the ox was as big as that.

The little frog looked and thought for a minute. "Bigger, Father, bigger," he replied, shaking his head.

So the father frog took a deep breath, and blew himself out, and blew himself out, and blew himself out... and he swelled and he

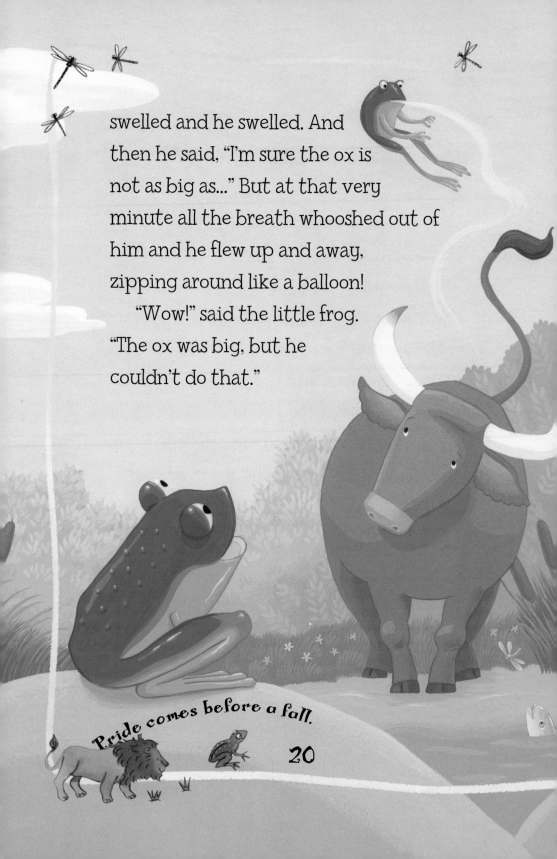

swelled and he swelled. And then he said, "I'm sure the ox is not as big as..." But at that very minute all the breath whooshed out of him and he flew up and away, zipping around like a balloon!

"Wow!" said the little frog. "The ox was big, but he couldn't do that."

Pride comes before a fall.

The Fox
and the
Grapes

It was a hot summer's day, with a gentle breeze rustling the leaves of the trees and the bees buzzing lazily around the nodding flowers in the meadows.

A fox came strolling through an orchard, humming happily to himself, when he suddenly noticed a bunch of juicy grapes just ripening on a vine. The fox licked his lips. "Those delicious grapes would be just the thing to quench my thirst," he said to himself.

But the only problem was, he couldn't

reach them. The vine was hanging on a branch way up overhead.

Nevertheless, the fox was determined to have the grapes for himself. He stepped back several paces, took a run up and jumped as high as he could – he just missed.

"If at first you don't succeed, try, try, and try again," said the fox, turning round to try again. "One... two... three..." he counted and he was off – jumping up even higher than before. But again, the fox could not reach the grapes.

Again and again he tried to reach the tempting morsel, until he was even redder in the face than usual, and quite worn out. All the creatures in the orchard – from the worms to the bugs and the birds – were laughing.

At last, the fox had to admit defeat, and he gave up. As he walked away to the sound of

sniggering, he stuck his nose in the air and said, "I am sure they are sour, anyway."

It is easy to look down on what you cannot get.

The Gnat and the Bull

There was once a huge bull who spent his days grazing in a field. One day, a tiny gnat came along and landed on one of the bull's horns for a rest.

The gnat found the place to his liking, and remained sitting there for a long time. He was quite nervous, for he knew that if he bothered the bull, the massive creature could kill him with a flick of his tail. However, as the bull had not said anything, he decided to boldly stay as long as he could.

Finally, the gnat had rested enough and was about to fly away, when he politely asked the bull, "Do you mind if I go now?"

The bull merely raised his eyes and said without interest, "It makes no difference to me. I didn't notice when you arrived, and I won't know when you leave."

We may be more important in our own eyes than in the eyes of others.

25

The Lion, the Mouse, and the Fox

A **lion was once asleep** when a mouse ran over his back. The mouse's feet tickled the lion and he woke with a start. He had no idea why he had been so suddenly awoken, and looked around to see what had disturbed him.

A fox lurking nearby had seen this happen, and he thought

it would be great fun to have a joke at the lion's expense.

"This is the first time I've seen a lion afraid of a mouse," said the fox loudly.

27

The lion was embarrassed, but tried to pretend he wasn't. "Afraid of a mouse?" he said. "Not I! It's his bad manners I can't stand."

If you take a small liberty with someone, it might cause great offense.

The Fawn
and his
Mother

There was once a deer who had a baby fawn. She cared for him well, and the fawn grew to be big and strong.

However he seemed to be afraid of everything. He would jump at the slightest rustle of a bush and start at the smallest snap of a twig. If he ever heard the barking of a dog – even in

29

the distance – he would be off as fast as his legs could carry him.

One day, the mother deer looked at her son and said, "My boy, nature has given you a powerful body and a stout pair of antlers. You could charge at anything with those and run them right through! I can't think why you are such a coward as to run away from everything."

Just then they both heard the sound of a pack of hounds in full cry – they knew that huntsmen must be coming.

"You stay where you are," said the deer. "Don't worry about me!" And with that, she ran off as fast as her legs could carry her.

No arguments will give courage to the coward.

The Bald Huntsman

There was once a man who had a fine head of hair. However, as he grew old it began to fall out, and he ended up entirely bald.

The man didn't like being bald and worried that people might think he looked better before. So he had a wig made, which was just like his own hairstyle, so the man thought no one would notice.

One day, the man went hunting with friends. He was wearing his wig as usual, with his hat perched on top. It was a windy day, so the man didn't get very far before a particularly big gust of wind caught his hat and carried it off — with his wig too. How all the other huntsmen laughed!

The man had a good sense of humor. He entered into the joke, and said, "If the hair that wig is made of didn't stick to the head on which it grew, no wonder it won't stick to mine."

Laugh and the world
laughs with you.

The Fox
and the
Mask

There **was once a fox** who got into
the storeroom of a theater. He strolled
round, examining the scenery, costumes, and
props, wondering what everything was.

The fox was delighted when he came across
what looked like a leg of chicken and a hunk of
cheese, but when he bit into them – yuk! He
found they were only made of paper and glue.

As he turned to see if he could find any real
food, the fox saw a face glaring down at him.
He sprang back in fear, but the face didn't

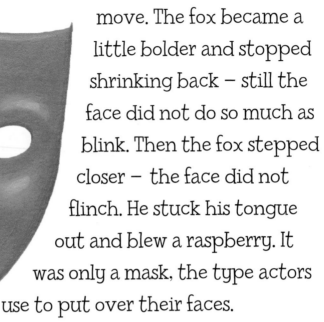

move. The fox became a little bolder and stopped shrinking back – still the face did not do so much as blink. Then the fox stepped closer – the face did not flinch. He stuck his tongue out and blew a raspberry. It was only a mask, the type actors use to put over their faces.

"Ah," said the fox, "you look very fine. It's a pity you don't have any brains."

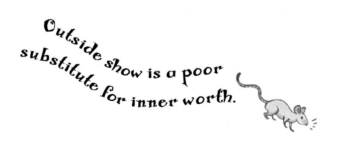

Outside show is a poor substitute for inner worth.

The Oxen
and the
Axletrees

Once upon a time, a pair of oxen were drawing a heavily loaded wagon along the highway. As they tugged and strained, a part of the wagon called the axletrees began to creak and groan with the strain. The more the oxen heaved and pulled, the more

36

the axletrees squealed and moaned.

This annoyed the oxen dreadfully. Finally, the temper of one snapped. With a great bellow, he turned round and looked back at the wagon, shouting, "Hey, you there! Why do you make such a noise when we do all the work?"

People who have the least to put up with often complain the most.

Hercules
and the
Wagoneer

There was once a wagoneer who was driving a cart with a heavy load. It had been raining and the road was muddy. The horse heaved the cart along, and the wagoneer guided him onto the firmest parts of the road.

Despite this, the wheels sank in the mud. The wagoneer set his shoulder to the cart and urged the

38

horse forwards, but the more they heaved, the deeper the wheels sank.

So the wagoneer prayed to the ancient hero Hercules, who was famous for his great strength.

"Hercules, please help me!" he cried.

"You called?" came a booming voice.

The wagoneer spun round to see a giant of

a man, with a lion skin wrapped round his shoulders. Hercules – for it was he – said, "Don't just stand there. I'm not going to do it for you! Set your shoulder to the wheel for one more push, and this time I'll help."

Fate helps those who help themselves.